P9-DYD-988

for Sale

Dragon
for Sale

by Marianne Macdonald
illustrated by Anne Kennedy

Troll

Chapter 1

About Emma

Emma Jones was lucky.

She had a mom and a dad and a room all her own, with a bed and everything to make her comfortable.

She had a closet full of toys and a new red coat. She had a bank shaped like an elephant, filled with pennies. She had eleven furry bears who sat on top of her dresser and came down whenever she wanted to play with them.

She had a big yard with a swing and trees and a shed full of interesting things.

She had a bicycle to ride. She had a best friend named Kerry.

But there was one thing Emma needed badly. She needed a dog to play with.

Emma told her mom, and then she told her dad. She explained about needing a puppy. She explained and explained.

Mrs. Jones said, "No!" Who would stay with a small puppy when Emma went to school and her parents were at work? Who would feed a puppy and let him out into the yard? Who would talk to a puppy when he felt lonely? "It wouldn't be fair," Emma's mom said.

And her dad just shook his head and said, "No, it wouldn't be fair."

When Emma went to bed, she dreamed she was playing with puppies all night long: big puppies, tiny puppies, black, gray, brown, white, spotty puppies. And when she woke up in the morning, she needed a dog more than ever.

Chapter 2

Eighty-Nine Pennies

Emma got dressed and put on her new red coat. She turned her elephant bank upside down and shook it until all the money fell out of the slot. Carefully she counted the coins. There were eighty-nine pennies. She put them into her little change purse and went downstairs. It was very early, and nobody else was up.

I'll go and get a puppy, Emma thought. *Just a very small puppy who won't be any trouble at all—they'll see! It will be fair.*

She let herself out the front door and walked quickly down the street. It was so early that nobody saw her go except Mr. Nowell, the milkman.

"Where are you off to, young Emma?" he asked.

Emma told him, "I'm going to get my new puppy."

"Oh!" said Mr. Nowell. "I'd like to meet him when you bring him home."

"Okay," Emma replied. She started to run toward the pet shop on High Street—the one with puppies and kittens in the window.

But she never got there, because she saw something else. It was on a corner, and it was a shop. Emma was almost entirely sure that a shop had never been on that corner before. But that couldn't be right, because it was an old shop—a very old shop. It was so old-fashioned that its front window was made of little panes of glass, so green and thick it was hard to see inside.

It's very strange that I don't remember this place, Emma told herself, and she pressed her face against the glass.

There was nothing in the window except a dusty sign painted on three square pieces of cardboard propped up side by side. Emma could just make out the faded words: MR. LYN'S PETS.

She put a hand on the doorknob. Her fingers tingled, like when your foot has gone to sleep and starts to wake up, but she paid no attention to that.

It was dark inside. The old window was very dirty, and the air was so dusty, it made Emma sneeze. She peered into the shadows. Right in front of her was a wooden counter with a birdcage on it. And in the cage there sat . . . an owl.

The owl blinked its great yellow eyes at her. Emma would have been afraid of its beak if the cage door had not been closed tight.

There were other cages hanging from the ceiling, with creatures rustling inside them. Emma was not tall enough to see exactly what kinds of birds were there, but they sounded big. More cages were lined up along the walls, and tanks held things that swam in dim greenish water.

And there, in the shadows behind the counter, was an old, old man.

Emma thought, for a moment, that he might be the oldest man in the world. He had long white hair and an even longer white beard. He wore a soft black cap and a long black coat with wide sleeves. He was puffing on a white curly pipe that sent streams of smoke swirling upward to hang in the shadows overhead. He had a thin white face with a sharp nose, and his eyes were the brightest, lightest blue. And when he suddenly stood up, Emma saw that he was very tall. His head seemed to be lost in the shadows and the smoke, though his blue eyes shone with an even sharper light than before.

But Emma was not at all afraid.

"Ummm," said the old man, and then "Hummmn, hummmn, chchch." He sounded like someone who had not spoken for a long time trying to get his voice working. When it was ready, he said, "And what can I do for you today, young Emma Jones?"

Then Emma felt just a little frightened. She said, "I haven't told you my name."

A chuckle seemed to start very far away and drift closer and closer. "Never mind," the old man replied. "It's written all over you. Now tell me why you've come into my shop."

Emma stretched up on her tiptoes to make herself taller and said, "I want to buy a puppy. I need a puppy very badly. I've brought all my money, Mr. Lyn."

The old man's face became serious. "No puppies," he said. "No puppies in stock. I have only one dog for sale, a watchdog. I don't think he's really the dog for you."

"Could I look at him, please?" asked Emma in a businesslike way. She sounded just like her mother when she was shopping for curtains.

"Can't you see him?" asked Mr. Lyn.

Then Emma saw the dog. He was in one of the cages by the wall. He was a very big, very black dog—almost as big as a pony. He raised his head from his paws and looked at Emma and yawned. Then he raised one of his *other* two heads from his paws and looked at her . . . and winked.

"No," said Mr. Lyn. "I'm quite sure that Cerberus is not the dog for you."

"I think my friend Kerry might be frightened of him," Emma agreed. "Even our milkman might not like him. But I'm not scared."

Mr. Lyn said, "I can see that. Now, shall we try to find out just which of my pets is for you?"

But Emma insisted, "I need a puppy. I don't think anything else at all is really for me."

Mr. Lyn looked at her sharply. He said, "You are wrong, my dear Emma. If there wasn't anything in my shop for you, then you would never have come in. Now what can it be? One of my rainbow fish? A bird, perhaps? A singing mouse?"

"I don't have much money," Emma said. She liked the idea of a singing mouse, but she thought it might be expensive.

Mr. Lyn's face brightened. "Ah! Exactly how much money do you have?"

Emma said, "Eighty-nine pennies."

Mr. Lyn was astonished. His pipe fell onto the counter (luckily without breaking). His black hat slid down onto his nose, so that he had to yank it back off his eyes before he could speak.

"Extraordinary!" he exclaimed, when he had recovered. He looked very carefully at Emma, beginning with her hair, down over her red coat to her shoes, and then up again to her face. "Well, there's no telling. . . . Are you sure you have exactly eighty-nine pennies?"

Emma was sure. She emptied her purse onto the counter, and the two of them carefully counted. There were eight piles of ten pennies. Then there was one pile with only nine. Mr. Lyn scratched his head and looked puzzled. Emma waited. She wondered what was so strange about having eighty-nine pennies. It

didn't seem like very much, now that it sat on Mr. Lyn's old wooden counter.

Mr. Lyn repeated, "Well, there's no telling. But I am a little surprised—I won't pretend otherwise."

He turned and stretched up to a shelf so high above the floor that it was entirely lost in darkness. He brought down a small, dusty, square cardboard box and put it on the counter just in front of Emma. There were airholes in the lid and a price tag that said 89 PENNIES in faded brownish ink.

Very carefully Emma lifted the lid. Inside was a bed of dry grass, with a little green "something" lying curled up tight. As she watched, the something stirred and began to unroll itself. There was a bony longish head with tiny knobbly ears. The body was round and hairless, with knobs of skin on the sides, two very short front legs, and two long back legs. Then a long, thin tail whipped out, and the little thing was stretching backward and forward—just like a miniature dog. It yawned

as it stretched, and a tiny pink tongue flickered in its little mouth. Then it opened its eyes and looked at Emma.

It had greenish-gold eyes, like a cat.

Emma said, "It's a lizard!" Then she asked, "Is it a lizard?" She put a finger out gently, wondering whether the lizard would bite. It climbed onto the finger and held on tight with strong, warm feet. It looked at her again.

Emma laughed. She said, "It likes me."

Mr. Lyn said, "Of course he likes you. He's for you, you see. Well, I never . . . Put him into the pocket of that cozy red coat of yours, and don't let him get cold on the way home. Don't let him get wet while he's so young either. He's only a baby. Of course, when he's grown up it won't matter."

Emma wondered what her new pet ate. Before she could ask, Mr. Lyn said, "Milk for the moment. Later, almost anything."

Before she had the chance to ask any other questions, Emma was out on the street again. The sunshine dazzled her after the darkness in the shop, so that for a moment she could barely see anything. But she heard Mr. Lyn's voice, fainter now, saying, "His name is Fair."

It seemed such a strange name for a lizard that Emma was going to turn around and go back to ask why he was named Fair. But by the time her eyes had adjusted to the daylight, the old shop was out of sight and she was halfway home.

Chapter 3

Fair Grows

All the way to her front door, Emma wondered whether she should have spent her money on the little lizard when it was really a puppy she needed. And yet, odd as it seemed, what she had bought was Fair.

When Emma's mother heard about Fair, she said, "What, a lizard? Well, I suppose it won't be as much trouble as a puppy." Then she said that Fair had better live in a box in the garage.

Emma hoped her mom would change her mind. She showed her how very little Fair was, and what beautiful greenish-gold eyes he had, and how warmly and strongly his tiny feet would curl around a finger. Then her mother said he could live in a box in Emma's bedroom.

"But only if he doesn't smell," she warned. "If he starts to smell, he goes out."

Emma cupped her hands around Fair and said, "Oh, Mom! He doesn't smell at all!"

Emma folded a clean old dishtowel into a shoe box. She punched holes in the lid of the box. Fair curled up in his new bed. When Emma put her face down very close, she could see his sides moving in and out, very slowly, as he breathed.

After she had watched him sleeping for a while, Emma heard her mother calling her. Because it was Saturday, it was time to go shopping. Emma found one of the saucers left over from a doll's tea set she used to have, and she filled it with milk. She put it carefully into a corner of Fair's box. She put the lid on the box and slid it gently under her bed for safety. Fair did not stir.

When Emma and her mom came back from the supermarket, Emma ran upstairs and opened the shoe box. Fair was asleep, but the saucer was empty. Emma stroked his back with the tip of her finger. It felt rough. Just for a moment, she thought she heard a sound like a soft purr. Just for a second, she thought she saw a flicker of gold as though Fair had looked through one slitted eye. But he didn't move.

Sadly she said to Fair, "A puppy would play with me, you know."

Fair let out a tiny snore.

Sighing, Emma brought him another saucer of milk and then went to watch television.

When she was getting ready for bed, Emma heard a rustle and went to look in the box. The saucer was empty again. Fair opened his eyes halfway and yawned a wide yawn before he curled up even tighter.

Emma looked at him closely. The little curled-up ball was . . . bigger.

"You've grown!" she exclaimed, just as her mother came into the room to ask whether Emma had brushed her teeth.

Mrs. Jones said, "Lizards grow very slowly, my love. You mustn't expect to see much difference in him for a very long time."

"But I do see much difference," Emma told her, and she went downstairs to get some more milk and say good night to her dad.

"Fair's growing!" she said when he kissed her good night.

"Good," he replied. "Now, off to bed."

On Monday when Emma got home from school, Fair had emptied his saucer and was waiting to be fed. He was so hungry that he drank two saucers of milk and snorted for more.

On Wednesday, Fair was too big to curl up in the shoe box. Emma had to make him a bed in a carton from the supermarket. She got one of the soup bowls from the dining room for his milk.

On Friday, Emma came home from school and found that Fair had climbed out of his box and onto her bed, where he was sound asleep on her pillow.

He filled the whole pillow.

At suppertime, Emma's mom said, "We

seem to be out of milk. I can't think where it goes these days."

"Fair and I are drinking it all the time," Emma told her.

"Good for you," her dad said. "We'll order some extra." And he put out a note for the milkman that read: PLEASE LEAVE AN EXTRA QUART UNTIL FURTHER NOTICE.

On Saturday when Emma woke up, the first thing she felt was something hard and heavy lying on her feet. It was Fair. He was stretched out across the foot of her bed. When he sensed Emma watching him, he sat up and yawned. She could see little white points inside his mouth. His teeth were beginning to grow.

"You're teething," Emma said. "I wonder whether it hurts a lizard? Babies cry a lot when they start teething. Maybe I should buy you a teething ring?"

Fair looked at her. His greenish-gold eyes shone like little flames. He wagged his tail and cocked his head to one side.

"I don't think Mr. Lyn had any toys for you, but maybe my parents will buy you something at the pet shop on High Street," Emma told him. "There are rubber bones and bones made of cowhide and all kinds of things that are safe for puppies, so I guess they'll be okay for you too."

On Monday morning, Emma left Fair in her room with a big mixing bowl full of milk and his new rubber ring to gnaw if his teeth hurt. But when she got home from school, there was no milk left. There was no mixing bowl left. And the new rubber ring had been bitten right in half.

Emma looked hard at Fair, who was lying on her bed.

Fair opened one greenish-gold eye. He burped. Emma peered into his mouth. Now there were two rows of pointed teeth in his bottom jaw and two rows of pointed teeth in his top jaw. But there was no sign of the mixing bowl.

"I know you ate it," Emma said to him sternly. "You are a very bad boy."

Fair hung his head. Emma stroked his ears,

which had grown into fan-shaped flaps of silky smooth skin. She sighed. "I suppose you can't help it, you're growing so quickly. Mom says our milk bill is growing too."

Then Emma remembered something. Mr. Lyn had told her that Fair should drink "milk for the moment," but Fair wasn't so little now. He was as big as a dog. He was as big as the black Labrador that Emma used to talk to in the park near the school. Perhaps Fair could eat other things now. Not things like mixing bowls, of course, but grass, like a horse? Or scraps, like a pig?

While Emma was wondering, her mom came into the bedroom and saw Fair stretched across the bed. She blinked. She looked at Emma. She stared at Fair. She looked at him for a long time. She said, "I don't believe this."

"He's a very fast grower," Emma told her.

"But, Emma!" her mother said. "How big is he going to get?"

Then she spoke very quickly. "How can we afford to feed him?

"Where can we put him? He can't sleep in your room any longer.

"What if he bites?

"He'll have to go!"

Fair got to his feet. The bed creaked as he jumped down with a thump. He trotted over to Emma's mom and wound his fat, knobbly body around her legs. He gazed up at her with bright eyes, and he licked her hand with his rough pink tongue.

"Oh," she said, softening. "Well, he is rather sweet. And maybe when he stops growing he won't eat so much. But he can't stay in your bedroom! He's going to be *much* too big for that! He'll have to live in the garage after all."

"Only when I'm at school," Emma pleaded.

Her mother said, "Well . . . if he's good . . ."

That weekend, Emma's mom got some old pieces of wood and a hammer and nails and built Fair a very big bed in the back of the garage.

Meanwhile, Emma went around to all the

houses on her street and asked the neighbors to keep their scraps for her new pet.

Emma wanted to tell Mr. Lyn about how fast Fair was growing, but when she went back to the corner where the pet shop had been, she found wooden boards across the door. There was a sign that said: CLOSED FOR RENOVATIONS.

Fair just kept on growing.

Chapter 4

Fair's Surprise

On Mondays, Tuesdays, Wednesdays, Thursdays, and Fridays, when Emma came home from school, she would go say hello to Fair, who was always waiting for her. Then she'd have a snack. Afterward she would take Fair a chocolate cookie, and they'd play together.

Often they would go upstairs to Emma's bedroom, although the stairs were getting rather narrow for him. Emma would tell Fair about school as he lay on the bed and listened.

On Saturdays and Sundays, unless Emma had to go out, they would spend the whole day together. Sometimes they played under the trees in the backyard. But if it was raining,

Fair would get sad. Then they would go inside, and Emma would read him stories from her books. His favorite seemed to be the one about King Arthur and his knights. When she read it aloud, Fair made a rumbling, bubbling sound.

Every evening before she went to bed, Emma took two red buckets and stopped by the neighbors'. They filled her buckets with their stale bread and bacon scraps and potato peelings and other leftovers. Sometimes a big bone or a newspaper got in by mistake, but

Fair never seemed to mind. Once there was even an unopened can of baked beans that the little girl up the street had put into the bucket when her mother wasn't looking. Fair ate everything Emma put into the old wash tub in the garage.

One morning when Emma went to see Fair, the Joneses' car had no side mirrors and no antenna. Her dad searched for them, but they had vanished. After that, he left the car out in the driveway overnight. Mr. Jones thought that Fair had buried the car parts—the way a dog would bury a bone.

When Fair had grown to be as big as a Great Dane dog, Emma thought he was slowing down.

Then, when he had grown as big as a young calf, she thought he was stopping.

Then, when Fair was as big as a horse (if you didn't count his tail), Emma was almost absolutely certain he wasn't growing much anymore.

Emma's best friend, Kerry, came to see Fair.

She didn't stay for long. She said, "Yuck! It's ugly! It has too many teeth! It's going to bite!"

Fair didn't like Kerry. He looked sulky and burped. Emma giggled. "You give him indigestion," she said. And Kerry went home.

When Kerry had gone, Emma studied Fair. He had a bony head, like a horse, with ears that folded like fans, and beautiful eyes. His dull-green body had an interesting ridge on the top, with funny knobs just behind his neck. His long tail was strong and fine. He twitched it when he was unhappy and wagged it when he was glad.

Emma threw her arms around Fair's neck and hugged him. She said, "Don't listen to Kerry. You aren't even the tiniest bit ugly. But I think you'd better keep your mouth shut and not let anyone see your teeth, especially my mom."

Fair did keep his mouth shut when Emma's mother was around. So she never knew that Fair could chew up mixing bowls and cans of beans and pieces of car.

One Friday morning when Emma went to visit Fair, he did not get up to greet her. He lay flat on his bed. His ears drooped. His eyes were dull. His tail gave only the smallest twitch. He looked very unhappy.

Emma gasped, "Oh, Fair, what's wrong with you?"

Fair closed his eyes.

Emma touched his nose. It felt hot. She brought a bowl of cool milk and put it where he could reach it. Then she had to go to school.

When she came home later that day, the milk had not been touched. Fair was asleep. He didn't move.

At bedtime, Emma went to say good night to Fair. The milk was still there, and the scraps were still in his dish. Emma called her mom, who came and looked at the sleeping lizard. She said, "I won't bother to take his temperature, because I don't know what it ought to be. Did he eat anything that might have disagreed with him?"

Emma said she didn't think so. She didn't tell her mother that Fair had always been able to eat anything at all without getting even slightly sick.

"Well, keep him warm," her mom said. "If he isn't better by tomorrow, we'll call the vet."

Emma woke up very early the next morning, because she was so worried. She put on her bathrobe and went quietly out to the garage.

When she opened the door, Fair was awake. He looked different, and he was pulling at something on his side—something that looked like bits of old leather. It was skin! The old skin was tearing away in strips. Underneath there were new, green, wet-looking scales. They shimmered when Fair moved.

Emma sat down beside him and watched.

Fair pulled and tugged until the old skin was all off.

Then he ate it!

Then he waited.

Then he slowly stood up.

Then he began to move.

At first, Emma thought he had begun to grow again right in front of her eyes. But then she saw that the knobby things on his back were swelling. Fair shook himself. Two fins like sails rose slowly behind his neck, gleaming gold in the shadowy garage. They spread out suddenly from wall to wall, with a *whoosh*! Fair flapped his wings, and the wind they made knocked Emma over.

Fair folded his wings against his sides and looked at Emma. His eyes were like two golden flames.

Next he drank up the milk. Then he ate the previous night's scraps. And after that he nibbled the bowl.

"Stop!" Emma shrieked. "Bad boy! Wait a minute!" But

she heard his stomach gurgling and knew there was no time to waste.

Emma ran out of the garage. Mr. Nowell was just putting three milk bottles down on the front doorstep.

"Mr. Nowell!" Emma shouted. "Mr. Nowell, I need more milk than that. I need a lot more! Fair was sick, and now he's better, but he's really, really hungry. If he doesn't get something else right away, I think he might eat his bed!"

Mr. Nowell laughed. "Now, now, Emma! Is that the puppy you were going to introduce me to? I'll just come and meet him now, okay?"

Emma said, "He's not a puppy after all. He's a lizard, and he's so hungry I think he might eat you."

But Mr. Nowell said it would take more than a lizard to eat him. He marched into the garage with Emma close behind.

Fair stirred. He raised his head on his long neck. Then he got to his feet with a rustling sound and spread his wings in the dark garage.

He was very, very big.

Mr. Nowell stopped. Looking a little surprised, he turned to Emma and asked, "Where on earth did you get that fine young dragon? I see he's just shed a skin and found his wings. No wonder he's hungry! You stay

with him and keep him quiet, and I'll run and get a few bottles of milk."

He was back in just a minute with a plastic crate full of milk bottles, which he put on the floor next to Emma. Fair reached down. He began to eat the bottles, and the crate too. His four rows of teeth had no trouble crunching up the plastic and the glass. When they were gone, he began to lap up the spilled milk.

"Oh," Emma cried, "you'll have such a stomachache!"

"Don't you worry," Mr. Nowell said. "Dragons have wonderful digestion. I'd better just go and get some more milk. But this time we must pour it quickly into his bowl. I don't know how I'll explain that missing crate when I get back to the plant."

Emma and Mr. Nowell poured thirty-six bottles of milk into Fair's bowl—and then another twenty-seven. As fast as they poured, he lapped. Finally, he seemed content. He chewed up one last bottle that Emma hadn't noticed. Then he burped and put his chin on

his paws, and with a final rustle of his new wings, he fell asleep.

"Whew! That was hot work!" Mr. Nowell gasped.

He and Emma sat down beside Fair, opened the last two bottles of milk, and drank them, because it had been such very hot work.

Then Mr. Nowell stacked up the crates and carried them off in a pile. When he and Emma were back at the milk truck, he said, "I'll check on him again in a day or so. I don't suppose anyone's ever kept a Welsh dragon in London before. I'm afraid there may be some more surprises."

"What kind of surprises?" Emma asked.

Mr. Nowell looked at her thoughtfully. "There's no point in asking for trouble," he said. "I won't say any more. But if there are problems, you leave a note under your empty milk bottles, and I'll see what I can do." And off he drove with the empty bottles rattling.

Chapter 5

Fair Speaks

One evening, not long after Mr. Nowell's visit, Emma and Fair were playing together in the backyard. Suddenly, Tiger jumped onto the fence that separated the Joneses' yard from their neighbor's.

Tiger was a big orange-and-white-striped cat with only one ear. He lived two houses away with Mrs. White, but he wandered into everyone's yard. He chased the dogs, and he scratched the other cats. He thought that all the yards in the world belonged to him.

Tiger jumped down onto the flower bed. He strolled onto the lawn.

He saw Fair.

Tiger had never seen a dragon, but he was

not at all afraid. He arched his back and stiffened his legs. He fluffed his tail up until he looked as big as possible.

Then he began to sing. Tiger had a very loud voice that started in a growl and rose up and up into a wail. It meant: You get out of this yard or I'll scratch you into little pieces.

Fair looked cautiously at Tiger. He was certainly surprised. He stepped back. Tiger stepped forward. Fair took another step backward, and Tiger paced two steps forward.

Emma shouted at Tiger. Fair started to shout, too, but when he opened his mouth,

something strange happened. Out came a puff of smoke. It smelled very funny. Tiger hesitated. Fair cocked his head. He seemed interested in what had just happened.

Fair opened his mouth again. This time he burped.

A little stream of fire shot out at Tiger. It reached all the way to his nose and frizzled his whiskers. Tiger looked shocked. He let out a yowl of protest, and a second later he was nothing but a striped blur whizzing over the wall. Fair burped again, but Tiger was gone.

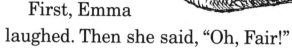

First, Emma laughed. Then she said, "Oh, Fair!"

She stared at her dragon. He stared back. He looked shy and proud. He puffed. A rosebush turned to ash. He blew. A heap of grass cuttings went up in smoke. He whooshed, and the corner of the shed glowed for a moment and then went all black.

"Stop!" Emma shouted. "Oh, Fair, don't do that! They'll be so angry if you burn the shed down!"

Fair stopped. But his greenish-gold eyes were thoughtful.

Then he did something else. Very slowly, very carefully, he spread out his wings. He began to flap them—up and forward, down and backward.

Emma watched, too worried to speak.

Fair stretched up on his hind legs, his head pointing toward the sky. His wings beat stronger and faster. He took two steps, and then his feet were off the ground. His wings caused a wind as he sailed over the fence. For

a moment, Emma thought he was going to catch Tiger and frizzle him up, but Fair was turning as he gained height.

Luckily, it was dark now. Nobody except Emma noticed a dragon in the sky. She held her breath. Fair wheeled and circled and tumbled through the air. He was having a wonderful time. He soared over the trees, over the yards, over the rooftops.

Suddenly, he was tired. It was his first flight. His wings felt heavy, and he landed with a bang on the very highest ridge of the Joneses' rooftop just beside the chimney. A loose shingle crashed to the ground.

"Emma, did you make that noise?" Mrs. Jones called from the back door.

"Not me, Mom," Emma called back. She didn't like to keep secrets from her mother, but she was afraid that if she came out and saw Fair sitting on top of the house, she might be very frightened.

Her mom continued, "Well, anyway, you'd better come in. It's time for bed."

"I'll just put Fair in the garage," Emma

said. Her mother nodded and shut the door.

Emma looked anxiously at the big shape, dark against the stars. She didn't know what to do. Was Fair stuck up there? Would he get frightened and fly away and be lost?

She called, "Bedtime, Fair!" just the way she did every night. The dark shape moved and grew, and Fair flew down and landed with a thump on the lawn. He folded his wings carefully along his back and followed Emma to his bed in the garage. She stroked his soft ears and told him he was a good boy. But as she closed the garage door, Emma was worrying.

She walked into the house and through the kitchen. Her parents were talking in the living room, and the television was turned down low. When Emma went in to say good night, she was almost absolutely certain she heard her father saying, "Well, you have to admit that the beast is much too big! It's too bad, but we are going to have to give him to the zoo."

She heard her mom say, "I just don't know how we are going to tell Emma."

Emma couldn't say anything. She went to bed and put her head under the covers and cried until her pillow was soggy.

A voice asked, "Who is Zoo?"

Emma was so startled that she stopped crying at once. She sat up. She could see everything in the room because of the light from the street coming through her window. Nobody was there, except for the eleven bears on top of the dresser, who never spoke.

The voice repeated, "Who is Zoo?"

"Where are you?" Emma asked, trying not to show she was frightened.

There was a puzzled silence. After a while, the voice said, "Bedtime, of course. You tell me it is bedtime. But who is Zoo?"

"Fair, are you talking to me?" asked Emma.

Fair said, "Of course I'm talking. Dragons can talk to people, you know. I am old enough to fly. My fire has come. I can talk now."

"But you're out there," Emma said. "And I'm in my room."

Fair said nothing. He seemed to be laughing.

"You're talking to me in my head," Emma said. It felt strange. But she wasn't at all frightened anymore.

Very, very quietly, in her bare feet, she tiptoed downstairs. In the living room, the television was still on. Emma went silently through the kitchen, into the backyard, and around to the little door in the side of the garage.

Inside, Fair was waiting for her. She could see him easily, because in the darkness his eyes glowed with a pale golden light. He was standing on his bed.

"Now, please tell me, who is Zoo?" Fair said.

"It isn't a person," Emma told him. She began to think of the zoo where she sometimes went with her mom and dad on the weekends. She thought especially of the lions and tigers in their cages, pacing up and down behind the bars. Then she thought of Fair in a cage, flapping his wings and not able to fly.

Fair could read the pictures in her head. He sat up on his hind legs and shouted, "NO!"

There was a puff of smoke that made Emma splutter. Fair said, "Dragons can't live in cages. Dragons die."

When Emma had stopped spluttering, she said, "Don't worry, Fair. I won't let them give you to the zoo." She felt his sadness, and it made her want to cry again. She sat down beside Fair. She leaned against his warm side. She could hear his fire bubbling and rumbling inside, and she knew Fair was right: He would die if he was put into a cage.

In a very tiny voice, Emma said, "You'll have to go away. You can fly now. Dragons in stories always live in wild places where there are mountains and caves. I understand what Mr. Nowell was trying to tell me. London is no place for dragons."

But Emma could tell that Fair was still worried. After a long silence, he said, "I don't know where to go. Is it far to the mountains? My wings are still very young."

But Emma didn't know.

Then she thought of what Mr. Nowell had said. She slipped back into the kitchen and found the pad her mother kept for writing out shopping lists. She tore off a sheet of paper. For a while she couldn't think of what to say. In the end, she just printed the message HELP HELP COME TO THE GARAGE. And when she had tucked it under one of the empty milk bottles waiting for Mr. Nowell on the front doorstep, she went back to Fair. The two of them curled up together and fell asleep.

Chapter 6

Farewell

When Emma woke up, it was daylight and Mr. Nowell was there. He and Fair were looking at each other. You could see that Fair was speaking to Mr. Nowell inside his head because Mr. Nowell was acting as if something tickled. He kept rubbing his ears.

Just in case he didn't understand, Emma cried, "Mr. Nowell, Dad says that Fair has to go to the zoo, but Fair says dragons die in cages."

"Well, of course," Mr. Nowell said. "Anybody could tell you that! Now don't you worry your head, because I've got a plan. But first we'll have some breakfast."

Mr. Nowell went to his truck and brought back two crates of milk, and Emma emptied the bottles into Fair's bowl until he'd had enough. Then she and Mr. Nowell sat on the edge of Fair's bed, and they each had a bottle of milk, too, because it had been very hot work.

"Now," said Mr. Nowell while they were drinking, "I'll tell you what we'll do. First, we'll take all the crates out of the truck and stack them in here out of sight. Then we'll load Fair onto the truck. He'll have to curl up tight and stay very still. We'll cover him up with all the blankets from his bed, so that nobody can see him. Then I'll drive him out to the edge of London, and as soon as it gets dark, I'll point him toward Wales.

"He's a Welsh dragon, for one thing. And, besides, there are mountains in Wales, wild places where a young dragon can find his own cave and live very comfortably."

Mr. Nowell's expression was thoughtful and a little puzzled. He added, "Fair says he has a friend who lives in Wales—an old man with a long white beard and a pipe, who knows all there is to know about looking after young dragons."

Emma understood. "That's Mr. Lyn!"

Fair whispered, "Yes, Merlin, Merlin . . ."

Mr. Nowell carried all the crates into the garage, and Emma helped him stack them. Mr. Nowell shook his head when he saw them there. "My customers will be wondering where their milk is today," he said regretfully. "Ah, well, it can't be helped. An emergency is an emergency!"

Fair climbed into the truck where the crates had been and folded himself up. Then Emma and Mr. Nowell brought his blankets. They spread and tucked and turned Fair into a mound of old bedding. Nobody could have guessed he was a real, live, fire-breathing dragon going home.

Then Mr. Nowell shook Emma's hand and climbed behind the wheel, and the milk truck clicked and churred and set off down the street. For a long time, Emma could hear Fair's voice crying, "Farewell! Farewell!" But no one else could hear.

After they had gone, Emma went indoors all alone.

That afternoon, her mother asked, "Aren't you going out to play with Fair?"

Emma thought for a moment. Then she said, "He's gone. He was getting too big to stay, so I've given him back to the man at the pet shop."

Her mom looked surprised, but all she said was, "Oh! Well, it's for the best, I suppose."

The next morning, the rattling of milk bottles woke Emma. When she looked out her window, she saw Mr. Nowell loading yesterday's crates onto his truck.

Emma tapped on the windowpane.

Mr. Nowell glanced up at her and smiled broadly. He gave her the thumbs-up sign before hurrying off on his rounds.

At breakfast, Mr. and Mrs. Jones were listening to the news on the radio. Just as Emma came into the kitchen, the announcer said: "An unidentified flying object was reported last night over Birmingham. It was seen by dozens of people. Air force fighter planes followed the object for some time until it vanished across the Welsh border. Pilots described it as a long shape, pointed at both ends, with sails that glowed in the dark. Ministry of Defense officials say . . ."

Mr. Jones turned the radio off with a snap. "Nonsense!" He laughed. "Some people will believe anything!"

Emma smiled to herself and had extra jelly on her toast.

On Friday morning, the mailman brought a small package addressed to Emma Jones. It felt quite heavy. It didn't rattle, but when she opened it, inside was a box full of pennies. She counted them into piles: eight piles of ten pennies, one pile with only nine. As well as the coins, there was a scrap of yellowing paper with some writing on it in pale brown ink. The handwriting was very scrawly, but after she had puzzled over them for a long time, Emma was finally able to read the words: "Fair exchange is no robbery."

Emma folded up the slip of paper and put it into her pocket, but when she looked for it later, it wasn't there.

On Saturday morning, her mom said, "Come along, Emma. Today we're all going shopping together."

They passed the corner where Mr. Lyn's Pets had been and went straight to the pet shop on High Street. In the window there were three kittens playing. They walked past the kittens and into the store.

Inside, the shop was very bright. There were cages full of yellow canaries and green-and-blue parakeets, all singing and squawking. There were tanks where goldfish swam in green water. There was a glass cage full of mice.

At the back of the shop, there was a big cage with newspapers on the floor. In it was a fuzzy white puppy with a brown patch on his back and sparkling brown eyes. When Emma went over, he ran up and wriggled at her. She gave him a finger to nibble through the bars.

The pet shop owner opened the door of the

cage, and the puppy came out to Emma. He bowed his front end and lifted up his back end, tail wagging. He gave a very small bark. He was saying: "Let's play."

Mrs. Jones said, "Now, Emma. Summer vacation has started. I'm not going back to work afterward, because we are going to have a new baby in the fall. So now is the time to get a puppy. We can all take care of him while he's little and make sure he doesn't get lonely."

And Mr. Jones said, "If you like him, we can take him now."

Emma sat down on the floor. The puppy climbed onto her lap and tried to bite her chin. Emma stroked him gently and whispered, "Your name is Dragon."

Emma's mom laughed and said, "You don't want to encourage him!"

But Emma said, "Oh, dragons aren't fierce. They're really very nice—just a little wild."

And the four of them went home together.